– To Sammy and Annika, because everyone has a poo story.

ISBN 978-1-7352102-0-9
All rights reserved. First paperback edition, June 2020.
Visit kocreatebooks.com for permissions requests and more information.

Story & illustrations
©2020 Lori Kothe

kocreatebooks.com

Oh Poo!

A Cautionary Tale

Lori Kothe

It's Monday morning
and time for a walk.

Nature is calling.
Let's go 'round the block.

"Don't forget to bring a bag!"
Mom hollers from the door.

If only there were poopless dogs,
I'd love them even more.

I hold my breath and cross my toes
as we get near a tree.

Maybe I'll get lucky,
and today he will just pee.

Oh poo!

Here comes a turd.

But nobody saw it.
Nobody heard.

I will just leave it.
How will they know?

Everyone does it.
I'll just go with the flow.

People in winter
just let it all freeze.

Dogs do their business
wherever they please.

And poo in the desert?
Now that's hard to beat.

It bakes into dust
in the sweltering heat.

It's all organic!
What harm can it do?

Why does it matter?
It's one piece of poo.

Oh shoot,
It's half past eight!

I drop off my dog
and hope I'm not late.

I'll take the shortcut
across the grass,

and run like crazy
to make it to class.

I land at my desk
at the ring of the bell.

**That's when I notice
a really bad smell.**

I look at my friends
then down at my feet.

The worst has just happened.
It's right at my seat.

Everyone saw it.
Everyone knew.

I am the one
who has spread all the poo.

The teacher just smiles
and makes a quick call:

"CODE BROWN IN ROOM TWO!"
I hear down the hall.

The custodian arrives
and starts clearing the scene.

"Let's take this outside,
 and I'll spray your sole clean."

"This isn't the first time.
It won't be the last."

He says as he turns on the hose
with a blast.

"Your story's unpleasant
but I've seen much worse.

There's one thing in common:
the mighty poo curse."

"When your bike rides right through it
and makes a brown splatter,

it sticks to your pants
like chocolate cake batter."

"Or out on the field
when you run for the ball,

then realize it's not mud
that softened your fall."

"The stories are different,
but you're never the same.

**You see that together
we're all in this game."**

He turns off the nozzle
and hands me my shoe.

I thank him and head back
to room number two.

I can't believe it!
How can this be?

Why did the poo curse
just happen to me?

I stare at my shoe
and my heart starts to pound.

I think of my dog poo
that's still on the ground.

It's the end of the day
and the tree is in sight.

Maybe there's still time
to make things be right.

**The poo that I left
is no longer there!**

I wonder what story
that poo has to share.